characters created by

lauren child

I've won,
NO I'VE
WON,
No I've won

PUFFIN

Text based on script written by Dave Ingham

Illustrations from the TV animation produced by Tiger Aspect

PUFFIN BOOKS
Published by the Penguin Group: London, New York, Australia,
Canada, India, Ireland, New Zealand and South Africa
Penguin Books Ltd, Registered Offices: 80 Strand, London WC2R 0RL, England

puffinbooks.com

First published 2005
Published in this edition 2008
3 5 7 9 10 8 6 4 2
Text and illustrations copyright © Lauren Child/Tiger Aspect Productions Limited, 2005
The Charlie and Lola logo is a trademark of Lauren Child
All rights reserved
The moral right of the author/illustrator has been asserted
Made and printed in China
ISBN: 978-1-856-13187-2

This edition produced for The Book People Ltd,
Hall Wood Avenue, Haydock, St Helens WA11 9UL

I have this little sister Lola.
　　　　She is small and very funny.
　　When we play "Who can sit
still the longest!"
　　　　Lola **always** has to win.

Last time we played, Lola said, "I've won!"

I say,
"But I didn't move!"

Lola says,
"Yes you did! I've won!
I always win...
always,
always,
always!"

And then she says,

"I can run faster than a speedy, speedy cheetah, and I can stand on one leg longer than a flamingo!

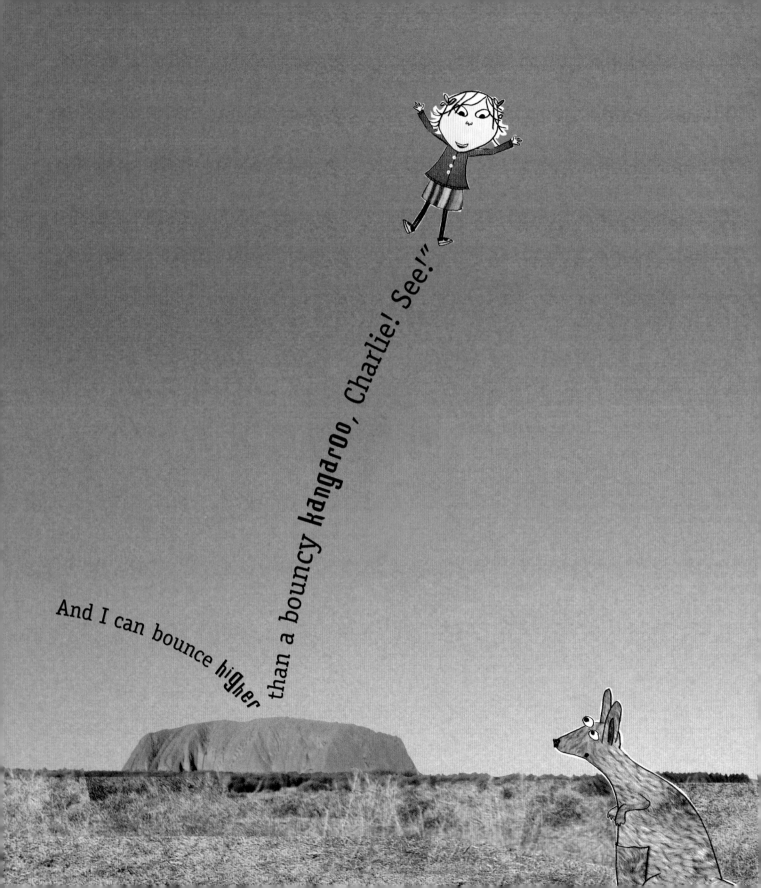

And I can bounce higher than a bouncy kangaroo, Charlie! See!"

Even when we're **drinking** pink milk,
　　　　Lola has to finish first.
　　I say,
　　"But do you have to **win** at **everything**, Lola?"

　　　　And Lola says,

　　　　　　　"Yep. I've won!"

So I say,
"How about a game
of spoons?"

I know I'm
better than Lola
at the spoon game.

But even so,
Lola says, "I'm winning!"
I say, "No you're not!"
She says, "I am."
I say, "Not!"

And then Lola
says,
"Aah, Charlie,
what's that?"

I look up at
the ceiling
and then when
I look back
at Lola...

her spoon has **definitely** moved!
I say,
"Lola, have you... **cheated?**"
But Lola says,
"Charlie, **I've won!**"

So then I say,
"Lola, you remember how to play **snap**,
don't you?
You need **two cards** that look the **same**,
then it's a **snap**."

Lola says,
"Yes, **two cards** that look
exactly the **same**,
then it's a
snap."

So I say,
"**five**."

So then I say,
    "How about a game of snakes and ladders?
You go
        up the ladders
                and
            down the snakes!
The one who gets to
                the top is the winner!
        Do you understand?"

Lola says, "I do understand, yes, Charlie!"

I roll first and I shout...

"Six!

1...2...3...4...5...6

and
up
the
ladder!"

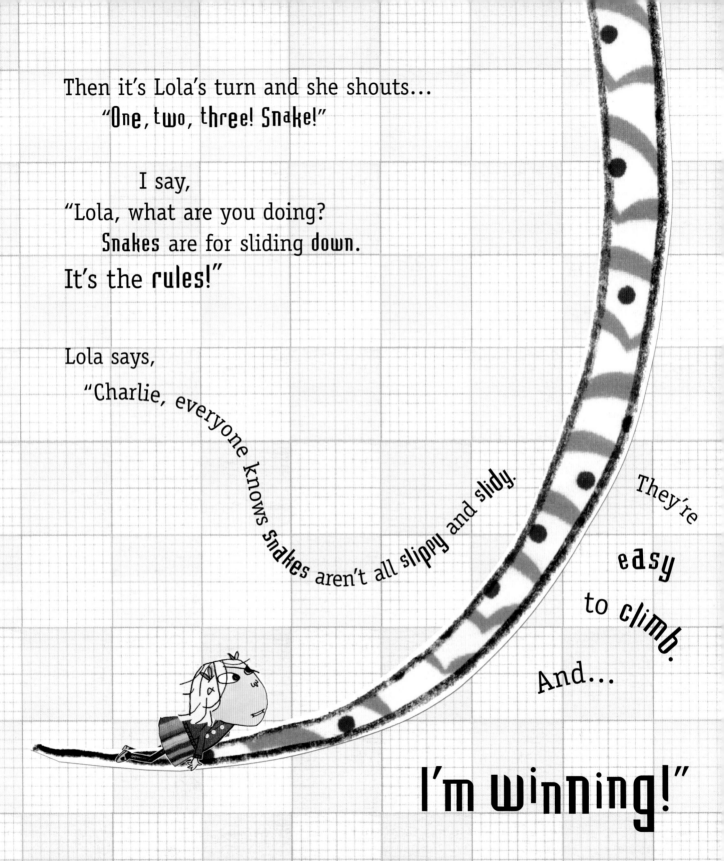

Then it's Lola's turn and she shouts...
"One, two, three! Snake!"

I say,
"Lola, what are you doing?
Snakes are for sliding down.
It's the rules!"

Lola says,
"Charlie, everyone knows snakes aren't all slippy and slidy.

They're
easy
to climb.
And...

I'm winning!"

Luckily I get another **six**, which means **up** a **ladder!**

But Lola says,
    "Charlie! Dad says you are not allowed to **climb** a **ladder!** Not until you are **twenty-three!**"

I say,
"Sorry. **Up** the **ladders** and **down** the **snakes**.

That's the rules!"

So Lola shakes the dice and says, "four!

1...2...3...4

snake!"

I say,
"Bad luck.
Now you've got to slide
down
all
the
way
to
the
bottom.
I've won!"

But guess what?
Lola pretends she's a **snake** charmer

and she charms the **snake** to the finish.

I say,
"But that's
cheating, Lola."

And she says,
"**I've won!**"

So I think of something
that Lola could
      never, never win!

When Dad takes us
        to the park I say,
"How about a race?
        It's once round
      the bendy tree!
Then two big swings
      on the swing!
Down the slide...
      and first one back
to the bench
      is
          the
              winner! OK?"

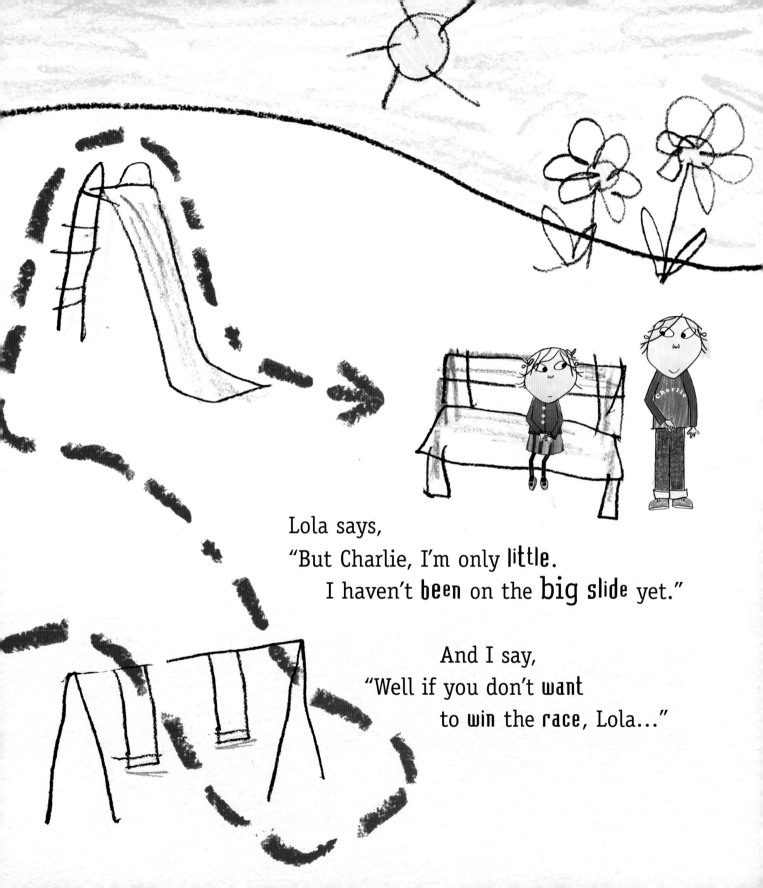

Lola says,
"But Charlie, I'm only little.
     I haven't been on the big slide yet."

And I say,
"Well if you don't want
     to win the race, Lola..."

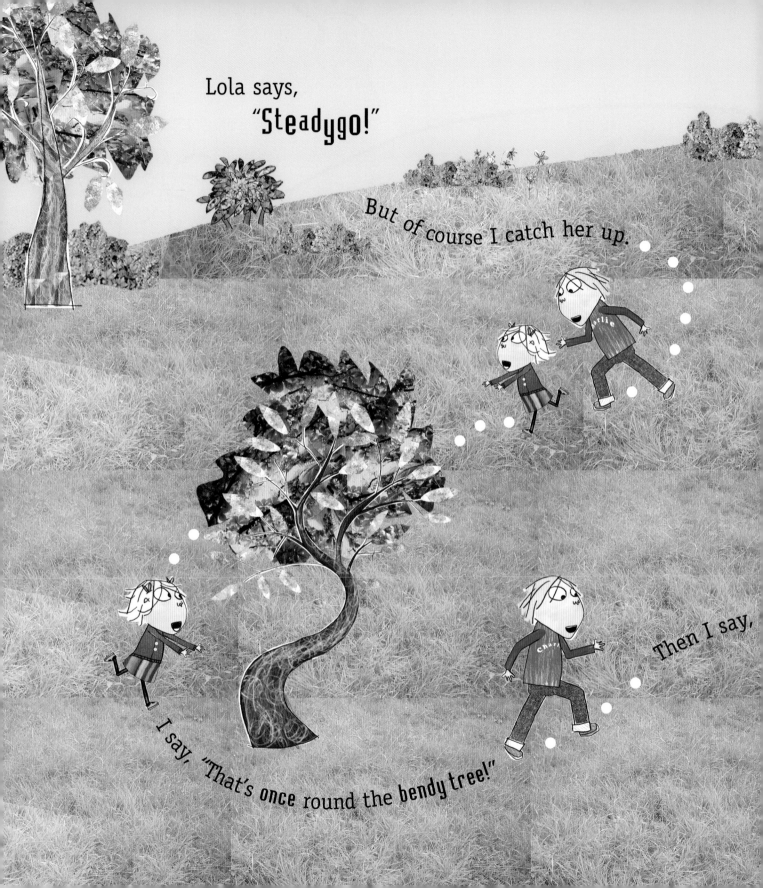

Lola says,
"**Steadygo!**"

But of course I catch her up.

Then I say,

I say, "That's once round the **bendy tree!**"

And guess what? I'm actually winning!

"And that's two big swings on the swing!"

But then Lola calls,
"Charlie!
Can
you
help
me?"

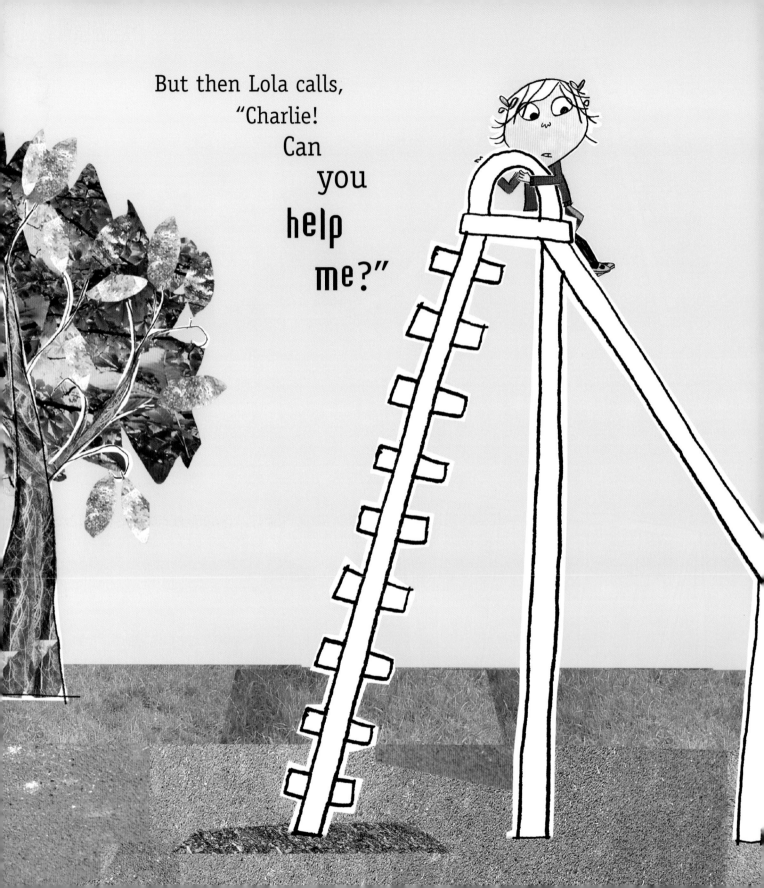

And even though
        I'm actually winning,
    I say,
"All right, Lola,
    I'm coming!
      Hold on."

We **w h o o s h** down the slide together.

Lola says,

**"Wheeeee-eeee!
I'm winning!"**

I say,

"Not for long!"

Then I say,
"And the
winner is...
me!

I've
won!

I've won!"

Then I remember Dad saying,
"Charlie, you must give Lola a chance,
because she's so **small**..."

And I say,
    "Are you all right, Lola?"

And do you know what Lola says?
    She says,

"That was fun!"

At bedtime, I say,
"Are you **asleep**
                yet, Lola?"

And Lola says,
        "Yes."

    So I say,
"How can you be **asleep**
if you are **talking** to me?"

She says,
        "I'm **sleep-talking!**"

    I say,
"The **first one** to
                fall **asleep** is
the **real winner!**"

And then Lola whispers, "Charlie? I've won!"
And I say, "No... I've won!"
"I've won!"
"No... I've won!"
"I've won!"